Cory Alexander

Followed

Who's Following YOU?

Copy Editor: Carra Robertson
Contributing Editors: Diana J. Jones, Kathryn Calvert
Cover Design: Bilal Abiyhasa
Book Design: Saravanan Ponnaiyan

ISBN-13: 978-0-692-97471-1

Harlem
Press,
LLC

www.HarlemPressLLC.com

🔍 Table of Contents   Cancel

TOP	PEOPLE	TAGS	PLACES

\#   **Chapter 1 – #WhosJohn**   pg. 01
177,700 posts

\#   **Chapter 2 – #PhoneDrama**   pg. 13
5,123 posts

\#   **Chapter 3 – #PerfectTiming**   pg. 19
1,947 posts

\#   **Chapter 4 – #No-Fi**   pg. 25
1,914 posts

\#   **Chapter 5 – #TheMeetUp**   pg. 33
1,657 posts

\#   **Chapter 6 – #Advice**   pg. 43
1,421 posts

\#   **Chapter 7 – #Finally**   pg. 51
1,018 posts

\#   **Chapter 8 – #T.H.I.N.K.**   pg. 63
957 posts

\#   **Chapter 9 – #ItHappens**   pg. 67
841 posts

\#   **Chapter 10 – #SquadGoals**   pg. 77
687 posts

\#   **Chapter 11 – #TheGame**   pg. 85
553 posts

\#   **Chapter 12 – #SoftMove**   pg. 91
462 posts

\#   **Chapter 13 – #ItHappenedAgain**   pg. 99
235 posts

#WHOSJOHN

The two BFFs got to their adjoining lockers at just the same time—in just enough time to pick up their books for first period. Brooklyn appeared to be in good spirits, as usual, but Vanessa didn't seem like her bubbly self.

"Hey, V!" Brooklyn had a habit of calling her friends by their first initial.

"Hey," Vanessa mumbled back, grabbing her algebra folder, avoiding eye contact with Brooklyn.

"So, what happened last night? Why'd you leave the Link so fast?" Brooklyn asked, referring to the online chat app that they frequented.

Vanessa didn't feel like talking to Brooklyn, but she knew Brooklyn would keep prying until she got an answer.

"I was tired." And on second thought, Vanessa continued, "And it felt kind of creepy that that guy John was only responding to *my* posts…AGAIN! I didn't like it when he asked for my number either. I mean, we don't even know the guy. I've never met him before. Don't you find that a little off?"

Brooklyn shrugged. "I don't know. He's super funny. And he seems cool." Teasingly, she added, "C'mon, V, get over yourself."

Noticing that Vanessa did not find that comment entertaining, Brooklyn quickly deflected, "Kidding. I'm just kidding. Honestly, though, what are you worried about?"

"I guess it's nothing." Vanessa gave her combo lock a twist and hurriedly began walking away. "I gotta get to math. Can't afford one more tardy from Stevens."

"Ok. See ya at lunch," Brooklyn called to her friend as she walked in the opposite direction towards her English class.

Just as Vanessa got to her math class doorway, a text appeared on her cell screen. It read, "Last night was lit. We should meet up 😊." Vanessa felt a pit in her stomach.

How did dude get my number? she thought.

Mr. Stevens was standing on the other side of the door pointing to his watch. Vanessa put her phone in her pocket and entered the classroom quickly. She couldn't risk being late. Besides, she didn't want to answer the text. She also hoped that ignoring John would send the message that she wasn't interested.

Some time later at first lunch, Jason and Bobby were at their usual cafeteria table with Brooklyn when Vanessa came over. "Hey guys, what's good?" Vanessa greeted everyone with a unique handshake.

"We were just talking about last night's chat. Brooklyn said you didn't like how John was feeling you," shared Jason.

"Yeah. Didn't you think he was kinda weird?" Vanessa asked, looking for approval from anyone at the table.

"I don't know," Jason responded with a shrug, looking around to see what the others thought.

"Who invited him to our Link thread anyway?" Vanessa continued. Everyone totally ignored her question.

"He seemed cool," Bobby added enthusiastically. "That joke he told was hilarious!"

"Yeah, he's a funny dude," Jason concurred.

"Who's funny?" asked Justin as he approached the table.

"John," Brooklyn answered.

"Who's John?" Justin asked.

"The new guy in our Link," Bobby countered.

"V thinks he's thirsty for her. She thinks he was showing her too much attention the last couple of days," Brooklyn added, rolling her eyes towards Vanessa. Brooklyn had always felt like Vanessa's the one who's gotten all the attention—probably because she did.

"Maybe we should be skeptical," Justin chimed in. "If we don't know John, why should we connect with him? There's a lot of trolls online, and some people aren't who they claim to be."

Everyone at the table sort of shrugged or shook their heads, neither agreeing nor disagreeing. He went on, "We need to be careful. Did you all hear what happened to Giselle from West Side High over the summer?"

In unison, the group all voiced a concerned, "No!"

Now they were paying more attention to Justin. "I'm surprised you didn't hear. It was all over FB."

"No wonder no one saw it," Harlem spoke up, finally taking his headphones off to join the conversation. "The only people on FB is your mama, my mama, and my aunts. If it ain't on BlastChat, it ain't news."

"What happened?" asked Bobby.

Justin began to tell the story, but just then, DJ came by with his music blaring, and the vibe totally changed. Jason started dancing, and the rest of the table started laughing and streaming Jason on their phones. Jason was "Mr. Charisma" and by far the best dancer in the school. He loved to party, and anytime was a good time for him to dance.

Vanessa was bummed because she really wanted to hear Justin's story about Giselle. She was definitely more weirded-out about "John" than any of her friends seemed to be. Maybe it was because she hadn't told anyone about the text he had sent her that morning. Vanessa kept thinking about the comments he had made to her, and specifically, the ones from last night. She wondered if the "Giselle story" was linked to her new creeper in any way.

Vanessa had always been super social, friendly, and very popular in school. She was the captain of the varsity volleyball team (the first freshman to ever hold the position). She'd been the cheer squad's most vocal leader, contributor to the school paper, and an all-around positive influence on school culture. Her peers considered her smart, funny, super pretty, and they'd often compare her to Zoey from the TV show *black-ish*.

Vanessa wondered if she was jumping to conclusions. After all, she'd always gotten a lot of attention for her looks and personality. She began to second-guess her instincts. *Maybe this isn't a weird situation. Maybe I'm overreacting to this whole John thing.*

Everyone continued dancing, posting clips, and having a good time. But Vanessa couldn't stop herself from thinking and wondering. She grabbed Justin and asked him if he could tell her the rest of the Giselle story. As he began to talk, the bell rang, reminding everyone that fifth period was about to begin. Justin started talking to Vanessa as they walked to their next class, but the hallway noise was deafening. Unfortunately, she couldn't hear a word he said.

As Vanessa moved closer to Justin to hear him better, Brooklyn immediately stepped in the middle. Brooklyn had a crush on Justin and couldn't risk competing with Vanessa.

Squeezing her way between them, placing her arms around their shoulders, Brooklyn yelled above the loudness, "Hey guys! Whatcha talking about?"

"I'm trying to hear the story about Giselle! Don't you want to know what happened?" Vanessa managed in a friendly tone even though she was getting awfully frustrated.

"If it was a big deal, I think we would have heard, don't you?" Then, Brooklyn murmured, "You just think every guy likes you."

"What did you say?" Vanessa asked Brooklyn, dismayed. She wondered if she had just heard Brooklyn throw shade at her, which was something that happened often—maybe too often lately. It hurt Vanessa's feelings because she was not a conceited girl, and, aside from Brooklyn, you couldn't find someone that thought she was. She knew she was popular, but she never flaunted it and was truly a modest person.

Brooklyn could be funny and was also considered cute by many of the guys. She had gotten used to being the center of attention at the school she attended back in New York, before she transferred. But here, she became simply the second most popular freshman behind, you guessed it…Vanessa. And clearly, often times, Brooklyn had trouble dealing with that. She could be considered sarcastic, mischievous, and a bit of an instigator. It's no surprise that she was often responsible for sparking school drama, and in many instances, for her own amusement.

"Nothing, Vanessa. I'm just saying, it's probably nothing." Brooklyn rolled her eyes while putting on her headphones and kept on walking down the crowded corridor. Justin also kept walking, attempting to make it to his class on time.

Vanessa called to him down the hallway from her classroom door. "The thing is, we don't know John, and he's in our Link!"

Vanessa took her seat in her forensic science class, but her head was definitely not there. Her brain was swarming with confusion as to why everyone seemed to think this whole John thing was OK. She also couldn't stop wondering what Justin's story might have been about; her thoughts were racing. Vanessa barely paid attention to Ms. Washington's lesson.

As the school paper's lead journalist, Vanessa's natural inclination to question things worked to her advantage. It was a gift and a curse. It served her well at school, as teachers felt her questions led to constructive in-class dialogue. But all the questioning was draining on her parents who thought it was cute when she seven, but tormenting by the age of 14. Then again, the apple didn't fall far from the tree.

Vanessa was assumed to have gotten her inquisitive ways from her parents. Her mother, Diane, was a social worker with a Ph. D. in Marriage and Family Counseling and had served the community for 20 years at the Department of Family Services. Her father, Marcus, was a local veterinarian who built his career on research, authoring his findings in top industry journals, and doing pro bono work in some of the more disadvantaged communities.

Dwelling on the Link thread (and not on science), Vanessa once again thought about the text message she had received from John. She regretted not telling the others about the private message. At least then, everyone would have the full story of her suspicions—especially since it came from a blocked number, something that's never happened to her before.

Vanessa got so anxious in class that she impulsively took out her phone and started searching on FB for the Giselle story to see what she could find. The school's Wi-Fi blocked FB and most other social media sites that students liked to visit, and her service was painfully slow. The old wing of the school, which is where her forensic science class was located, had the worst cell service. It was a virtual dead-zone. However, Vanessa somehow had the administrators' Wi-Fi passcode. As she finished typing in the search bar, Ms. Washington walked by her row and caught her.

"Vanessa, please hand it over," Ms. Washington pointed to the cell phone. "You know you're not allowed to have your phone out, except in the cafeteria." Vanessa gave over the device and apologized.

"You know where you can pick it up after school. Thank you." Ms. Washington was going to give it to the Vice Principal and Vanessa would have to get the phone from him after school.

From then on, Vanessa barely paid attention to the rest of the lab experiment, which was typically her favorite part of the class. The only way she could get her phone back was if one of her parents came to pick it up. She also knew what her parents expected of her, and this certainly was something that was going to disappoint them and warrant some sort of discipline.

1. Have you ever had a rocky friendship like the one Vanessa and Brooklyn have? What made it good? What made it difficult?

_____

_____

_____

_____

2. Why do you think you stayed friends for as long as you did?

_____

_____

_____

3. Are there things you look back on and think you could have done differently to have made the friendship better? If so, what were they?

_____

_____

_____

4. Have you ever felt uncomfortable on social media because of something posted about you from someone you didn't know? If so, what did they post, and what did you do about it?

_____

_____

_____

2

#PHONEDRAMA

Vanessa was frustrated that Mom or Dad would have to come to school and meet with Vice Principal Williams. She got mad at herself for getting obsessed with this whole Link thing. Self-doubt crept into her thoughts again. *Maybe John is OK. I really shouldn't think the worst of people.*

At the end of science class, Vanessa went straight to the next period, which was gym. Bobby, a member of the JV basketball team, was already there and approached Vanessa while dribbling a basketball. He was super laid-back—and was also considered a major flirt by most of the cheerleading squad.

"I hear you think John from our Link has something to do with Giselle."

"Where did you hear that?" Vanessa asked, surprised, especially considering she hadn't told anyone that she suspected there was a connection. Coincidentally, at that moment, Justin strolled out of the boys' locker room with his gym gear on. Bobby didn't need to say anything. He answered her question by looking directly at Justin. Vanessa also looked at Justin, with disgust, and proceeded to the girls' locker room.

"Why'd she look at me like that? What did you say to her?" Justin asked Bobby with a disdainful look.

"Nothing, I just asked her why she thought Giselle and John are somehow linked," Bobby replied in defense.

"I told you to keep your mouth shut. Now she thinks I don't believe her!"

"Well, do you?" Bobby exclaimed.

"You never know. What if? That's all I'm saying. You never know." Justin paused and then questioned Bobby, "So, do you know John?"

"No, but he seems cool. He's funny, and he posts some awesome stuff."

"Stuff like what?"

"Pics of where he lives… what he's eating… places he's visited… stuff like that."

"OK, cool." Justin was only marginally satisfied with Bobby's responses. Even *he* was starting to feel a little suspicious. "Has anyone seen a picture of this John guy?"

"I dunno," Bobby replied after giving it brief thought. "I know I haven't."

Justin pressed on. "Isn't that strange?"

"Not really. People choose chat icons of whatever. Mine is the Laker logo and that doesn't make me dangerous or prove that I'm hiding something." Bobby was visibly getting uncomfortable with the line of questioning.

"Well, I am beginning to think that Vanessa *may* have a point. I mean, how do we know if John is even our age?"

"Seriously? He talks about stuff we like… and stuff we like to do," Bobby replied assertively, feeling like he came up with a good enough response. Now taking the offensive, Bobby decided it was his turn to ask a question. "OK. So, how would John know all that stuff if he wasn't our age?"

Right before Justin had a chance to respond, a volleyball flew out of nowhere smashing him right upside his head. He looked to see where the ball had come from and noticed Vanessa smirking from the other side of the gym. He rubbed his temple and waved off the "going nowhere" conversation with Bobby.

Justin walked over to Vanessa to apologize for mentioning her concerns to Bobby. "I'm sorry, Vanessa. All I did was mention that you were worried." With genuine intent, he added, "I want you to know that I take your feelings seriously."

There was an awkward silence between the two friends— until Justin swiftly changed the subject.

"Hey, I heard Ms. Washington took your cellphone."

"The worst. Word gets around fast, huh? I wanted to look up the Giselle story. I was anxious to find out the details, but then Ms. Washington saw me. Now my parents are going to get called to come get my phone. Ugh."

"Yeah, that whole cellphone policy is so lame."

"True. So, tell me the story already!" Vanessa insisted, giving Justin her undivided attention.

"Well, I heard from Big Nate, who goes to West Side High, that there was this girl named Giselle. She met this guy in the Link. I think Nate said it was a cheerleading Link. I can imagine the amount of dudes that go there to try and hook-up. Then, after a week of messages back and forth, he asked to…"

Their conversation was interrupted by Coach Cal's whistle. Coach Cal was serious about his P.E. class. He didn't hand out good grades just because students changed into their gym clothes. They actually had to exercise. "Gentlemen, please grab the mats and start with some crunches. Ladies, you'll be running the perimeter of the field today. Two miles. Timed."

Many of the girls moaned and complained, and several of the guys laughed teasingly.

"I don't know what you gentlemen find so funny," Coach Cal interjected. "Tomorrow, you will be finding yourselves on the field—doing three miles." Most of the girls laughed, and even many of the boys were amused. Vanessa didn't find any of this entertaining. All she wanted to do was hear the Giselle story. No such luck. The coach blew his whistle again and gestured for all the girls to file out towards the track.

By seventh period, Vanessa had more questions than answers. Even worse, word was already getting around that her friends thought she was a conspiracy theorist. It was tough to know exactly what everyone was saying because she didn't have her phone to see and read first-hand. Apparently, Brooklyn had been posting comments about Vanessa not trusting people, and Vanessa thinking people she's never met were creeps, and that Vanessa now hated chatrooms, and a whole bunch of other stuff—stuff that Vanessa couldn't respond to without her phone—which maybe was for the best.

Vanessa didn't want to have a social media argument with Brooklyn. She had learned from experience how irresponsible it can be and how crazy and out-of-hand things can get. She was disappointed that this had now turned into "sort of a big thing." She also felt bad that no one else had the same suspicions about John. And, the one person she thought would have her back, Justin, was making fun of her by talking to Bobby, someone that didn't take stuff seriously. Based on the social media attacks from Brooklyn, Bobby's comments, and her own phone drama, Vanessa began wondering if she could have handled things differently.

1. When was the last time you felt your friend(s) didn't have your back? How did that make you feel?

_____

_____

_____

2. Have you ever been in an online disagreement? Did it get resolved? If so, how was it resolved? If not, why do you think it wasn't?

_____

_____

_____

3. If you could go back in time, what would you have done differently?

_____

_____

_____

#PERFECTTIMING

Towards the end of seventh period, Vanessa was incredibly emotional. She started tearing up and asked to go to the bathroom. Leaving the class feeling lonesome (and confused about her feelings), she went to her guidance counselor's office. Mr. Jones was on the phone, but when he saw Vanessa in his office doorway, he waved, placed his hand over the receiver, and mouthed the words, "Give me one minute."

Vanessa sat down to wait, and just as she figured out the best way to explain the situation, the bell rang for her next class. *Wow, my timing is just terrible today.*

Feeling dejected, she left Mr. Jones' office waiting area and forged on to her last class of the day. Still in search of clarity, Vanessa sat in her creative writing class trying to figure out what to do next. It was essay-writing day and the assignment topic was on the board. Her classmate Aaron handed her one of the tablets from the computer cart. Rather than writing her essay on the tablet, Vanessa used its internet feature to once again search for the Giselle story. As she found what appeared to be the story on some random site she didn't recognize, believe it or not, the fire alarm went off. Instantly, she thought, *Is this some kind of cruel joke?*

Everyone rushed out of the class and onto the football field. As the students gathered into groups by class, Vanessa spotted Justin about 20 yards away. She attempted to make her way over to him when her teacher, Mr. Lloyd, shouted for her to stay with the class. "Vanessa, you know this is serious. Everyone in my class is under my care!"

Frustrated, thinking about how her father was going to handle having to leave work early to pick up her cellphone, Vanessa stood quietly and waited for the Head of Security, Ms. Vonda, to give the "all clear" signal so that everyone could come back in from the drill. As the students returned to their classrooms, Mr. Lloyd explained the importance of fire safety and his responsibilities during a fire drill. "I'm responsible for everyone in my class," said Mr. Lloyd, looking directly at Vanessa. She really didn't need that; she already had a lot on her mind.

"Yes, Sir," everyone shouted sarcastically.

Vanessa, however, was more focused on rebooting her tablet. However, before the home-page screen even came up, her name was called over the loudspeaker. "Vanessa James, please report to the Vice Principal's office and bring your belongings with you." Many in the class snickered, knowing what had happened to her phone. Vanessa gathered her stuff and headed to the VP's office.

There, in the office, Vice Principal Williams and her father sat talking about the reason her phone was confiscated. As she walked in, her dad was shaking his head slowly back and forth. "I'm really disappointed in you. Why would you have your cellphone out during class? You know the rules, and you certainly know what we expect of you in school!"

Vanessa attempted to respond, but her father cut her off. "We'll talk about this later. Just so you're aware, I told your mother, and she's equally disappointed."

The car ride back home was booming with silence as Vanessa was trying to figure out a way to tell her dad what was going on. The only problem was that Vanessa had been on her phone in the Link beyond the time she promised to turn off social media. If she told her Dad, and he looked at the last entry time, things would just go from bad to worse. Therefore, she decided to adopt another strategy.

Mom came home after work, and together with Dad, the two parents questioned their daughter as to why she had her phone out during class. Vanessa omitted all of the true details as to why she pulled out her phone and instead chose to go with a frivolous excuse. She mentioned that a friend had tagged her in a photo and she wanted to check it out. She listened to them lecture, nodding in agreement to appease them, all the while thinking about how she would get back online to research the Giselle story.

Vanessa listened to her parents explain the consequences with half-an-ear. She figured that part of her punishment would be no cell for the weekend, which, of course, for her would feel like forever. As soon as they finished speaking, she jumped up and said, "You're right. I apologize for being so irresponsible. I have no excuse. I love you, and I have to own up to my poor judgment." Vanessa gave them both a kiss and darted to her room. Her parents shot each other a quizzical glance.

"That was easy," her mom remarked.

"Too easy," her dad concurred, with a raised eyebrow.

HOW ABOUT YOU?

1. What is your school's cellphone policy? Do students honor it?

_____

_____

_____

2. Do you think the policy is fair? If you could create the policy, what would you think it should be?

_____

_____

_____

3. Do you think students' cellphones are helpful or distracting in class? Please explain.

_____

_____

_____

4

#NO-FI

Once in her room, Vanessa booted up her laptop. As she put in the password, it denied her every attempt. On the third try, it went into security mode and instructed her to try back in 30 minutes. *OMG, what now?* Apparently, Mom had changed her password once she heard what had happened at school. Vanessa's punishment was a ban on internet access, not just cellphone use.

All she could think was, *What am I going to do now?* Vanessa went back down to the kitchen to try to reason with her parents.

"Mom, Dad… I don't understand." That was the best she could muster.

"I can explain, again, sweetheart," her dad said in a calm tone. "This will be a text-free, digital-free, internet-free weekend."

"I think you guys are overreacting. This isn't fair!"

Her father looked over at her mother. "That's why it was so easy. She wasn't listening."

"No, I was listening. It's just that, that, …it's just that, I was doing important research," she stuttered, finally settling on a new course of reasoning.

"What were you researching? Let us be the judge of how important it was," her mom chimed in.

"Well, it's just that, I needed to know something and I…" Vanessa was searching for a way to explain, without saying too much. "…It was important to get the information as soon as possible."

"What information?" her dad pried.

"Well, uh…" she looked at the ceiling for an answer. She found one. "Cindy and I have a project due!" Vanessa continued with renewed confidence and enthusiasm. She was sure her parents would approve of this reasoning since it was schoolwork. "I think it would be wise to start working on it now! Don't you agree?" Mumbling under her breath, Vanessa added, "Since there's nothing else to do."

"Well, that is a wise idea, but, unfortunately, it's become a digital-free weekend. I'm sorry. I can't be sure you won't visit a wink-chat or watch videos on YourTube when you should be working on the assignment."

"It's a Link-chat, Mom, and it's YouTube," Vanessa scoffed, shaking her head.

Her mom smiled as if to say, "I was just joking, I knew that!" "Whatever the case, you have your punishment. Start by reconnecting in person and give your thumbs a break. You know, back in our day, group chat meant hanging out in person and talking. It's quite an interesting concept."

"Yes, I'm sure it is, Mom." Vanessa left for her room, dispirited, also feeling the need to get out of there before her mom started a deeper "back in MY day…" story.

Once again, in her room, Vanessa plunked herself onto her beanbag, wondering what her next steps should be. *I need to find out what happened with Giselle!*

As her brain swirled for a solution, Vanessa remembered that she had an old tablet—somewhere! She had it before she got her Smartphone. And, it was on the family plan, too. *I doubt they remembered to close the account.*

Vanessa felt confident that she'd get to the bottom of this shortly. She found the device in the back of her closet under boxes and boxes of rarely worn sneakers. Vanessa was a sneaker-head, and she bought and resold sneakers. (She was quite the young entrepreneur.) With renewed vigor and a sense of false pride, she felt victorious, until she tried to power-up the device and found the battery was dead. She looked everywhere for the old charger, to no avail. Then, she remembered that there'd probably be one downstairs in the utility drawer.

She figured that if she went in search of the charger and her parents noticed, they would remember that she had something that got her online, or at a minimum, question what she was looking for.

I have a better idea! Vanessa declared to herself.

"RILEY!" she yelled. As her 11-year-old brother approached, she put on her best big-sister-happy-to-see-her-little-brother face. "Do me a solid lil' bruh. Can you get the charger for this tablet from the utility drawer in the kitchen? It's with all the old chargers. Love you. Go, go, go!"

"Seriously, Big Sis? One, why are you asking me to get it for you? And two, what's in it for me? I heard about your little cellphone thing at school, so I'm kind of figuring if you're asking me to get your charger, you're avoiding Mom and Dad. That has to be worth something," he said, smiling from ear to ear, crossing his arms.

"Come on, Riles, whatever happened to love?"

"Love ya," Riley responded, "but what's love got to do with it?"

Vanessa socked Riley in the arm. "What do you want, you little…?" Vanessa caught her words, but not her physical impulse to punch her little brother in the arm.

"Ah, ah, ah… be nice," her brother scorned her, knowing he had the upper hand—while rubbing his arm from the pain.

Vanessa was fuming. She felt that Riley didn't know what was really going on and was just squeezing her in the most inopportune time. Well, inopportune for her. "What do you want, you little bugger?" she asked with her teeth clenched.

"Well, I'm not particularly interested in cleaning the bathroom. And, it's my turn."

"OK," agreed Vanessa with disgust, but without hesitation. "Done. I got you. Just go grab my charger and I'll clean the bathroom. Fine. Yes, I got it—go, go, go."

"I can't tell you how happy I am to help," Riley said with a Cheshire cat smile as he dashed down the stairs. Vanessa listened with anticipation at the top of the staircase.

"Hey, Mom. Hey, Dad," Riley greeted them as he passed.

"Hey, Riles, whatcha up to?"

"Ah, nothing much, just grabbing the charger."

"It's on the table right there," Mom responded.

"No, I need the old one, from the utility drawer."

"Oh, good luck finding anything in that mess-of-a-drawer."

Cripes! Why did Riley say that? They're going to wonder why he would need an "old" charger! That's all Vanessa could focus on.

Riley hurried back up to Vanessa's room and gave her the charger. "Thanks, bugger, I owe you one."

Riley smiled, "I know. And don't forget to scrub the toilet extra hard. You be dropping bombs."

Vanessa grabbed the charger and kicked Riley out of her room as he laughed hysterically at his poo remark. She plugged it in and after thirty minutes of charging and another thirty of trying to remember her old passcode, she unlocked the device. "System Update Required," it read.

"Noooooo!" she shouted, and thought to herself, *Oh boy, just one obstacle after the next!*

Her dad called from downstairs, "Everything OK up there?"

"No! I mean, yes! I'm OK... I just banged my toe on the dresser," she yelled back. Vanessa made a mental note to take a few deep breaths and chill out before she made things worse. The tablet finally updated the operating system. "Yes!" she whispered with enthusiasm, along with doing a little celebratory fist pump.

Vanessa started to search, but as soon as 9 p.m. struck, the internet connection shut down. *Ugh!* Just then, she remembered that Mom and Dad controlled the internet usage from an app on their phones. *I totally forgot about the "OurPact" app.*

Vanessa's parents had downloaded this internet-blocker after viewing the documentary *Screenagers* at the Town Hall meeting. All the devices Vanessa could've used were simply locked. Vanessa became more aggravated. *Do I dare ask Riley for another favor? What will that cost me? And is it even wise to try to outsmart my parents any further?*

Weighing her options, Vanessa decided it would be best to honor her parents' rules and rebuild some trust. Having no internet access made for an early Friday bedtime—the earliest she could ever remember. Since all her friends were online, and she had no way of joining them, she cleaned the bathroom and went to sleep.

HOW ABOUT YOU?

1. When was the last time you didn't tell the truth? How come?

_____

_____

_____

2. Do you ever admit when you are wrong after being caught or disciplined?

_____

_____

_____

3. Do your parent/guardian(s) admit when they're wrong? If so, how does that make you feel? If not, how does that make you feel?

_____

_____

_____

5

#THEMEETUP

The next morning, Vanessa woke up early, excited to connect with her friends and catch up on all that had happened the previous night, which she had missed out on. She called Brooklyn and left her a voicemail. Seconds after leaving the message, Brooklyn called back, yelling, "Hey! Someone called me from this number?"

"It's me, Vanessa!"

"V, where are you? What number is this?"

"It's my home phone number."

"You have a home phone?"

They both laughed. "My parents took my cell for the weekend, so I'm faded. What's up later today?"

"We'll be hangin' at the Park Street Mall in Ocean View Commons."

"I love that mall! I'll meet you there. What time?" Vanessa inquired.

"Bobby and Jason are coming by to get me. We should be there around one."

"OK, I'll see you then!" Vanessa plunked down the phone receiver and jetted to her room to go get ready.

Vanessa was full of anticipation to meet her friends and catch up on all she had missed from the Link. She told her parents where she was going, and off she went. In the food court, in front of their favorite donut spot, sat Brooklyn, Bobby, and Jason. "What's up, guys?"

"Everything," Jason responded with a grin from ear to ear. "You just missed a crazy night in the Link. Where were you?"

"I got punished for having my phone out in Ms. Washington's class."

"Ms. Washington is tough. She never lets you go to the bathroom, and she always gives homework," Brooklyn stressed.

"Yeah, she's a hard teacher. Oddly, though, I get my best grades in her class," Vanessa conceded.

"She gives homework every night," Bobby commented.

"Even on Fridays," Jason added. "Who gives homework on Fridays?"

Collectively, shaking their heads, everyone blurted out, "Ms. Washington," which, of course, was followed by group laughter.

"Has anyone spoken to Justin?" asked Vanessa.

"He was in the Link last night, but he was super quiet. John had everyone laughing and showed us some sick pictures of his house," Jason replied.

"It was dope," Brooklyn added. "His house is crazy."

"Justin was online and kind of stopped chatting once John came in," said Bobby.

"I don't know what's up with that," Jason added.

"Yeah. I don't know what's up with him," responded Bobby.

"Well, since Vanessa has a problem with John, I think Justin has a problem with John, too! You know Justin has a major crush on Vanessa and whatever she says, he does," Brooklyn claimed.

Vanessa ignored her comments. She knew Brooklyn liked Justin, and responding back with a slick response wasn't as important as finding out what else had happened. Vanessa wanted to express her concerns to the group. She was about to "tell all" when, all of a sudden, Harlem yelled from the balcony, "Guys, what's uuuuup?"

Vanessa felt like no one was taking her concerns seriously. Maybe her best move would have been to just tell her parents. But the more she thought about it, coupled with the "John fan club" love from the rest of the guys, she instead became more indecisive. Her mind was swaying back and forth. Vanessa replayed the order of events in her head. *Yeah, he paid a lot of attention to me in the Link, he asked for my phone number, and then, he texted me from a blocked number.*

What she didn't know yet was that John had started following her on IG and liked all her pics. Paralyzed with uncertainty, Vanessa stopped speaking about John any further. She just planned to catch up on what she had missed last night and have fun with her friends.

That was her plan until about an hour later when Justin showed up at the mall. Justin greeted everyone and asked what they'd been up to since they got there. Vanessa was happy to see him, but she was uncomfortable talking to him about John because of Brooklyn's earlier comments. Furthermore, Vanessa was convinced that everyone had become a fan of John's, so anything she said would be seen as hating.

Against her better judgment, Vanessa, nonetheless, burst out, "Why didn't anyone invite John to the mall today?"

"I did," answered Brooklyn, probably way too fast, "and he asked if you were going to be here. I said I didn't know."

"I'd rather you not talk about where I will be and where I won't be to strangers," Vanessa snapped back.

Brooklyn rolled her eyes. "Oh yeah, I forgot. John's a mastermind criminal and a kidnapper." Everyone except Justin and Vanessa laughed.

"I didn't say that," Vanessa responded.

"What's up? Who's John?" Harlem asked, totally lost and feeling like he just walked in on the middle of a movie. He lowered his music to get a better understanding of what was going down.

"Vanessa felt this new guy John was a little thirsty in the Link the last couple of nights," Justin defended. "Since he's new to the thread and nobody really knows him, Vanessa is feeling a way about it. Remember we mentioned him yesterday at lunch?"

With a shrug, Harlem responded, "Naw, I was listening to the new mix me and DJ put together for the pep rally."

"So, what's exactly strange?" Harlem asked, looking at Vanessa.

"Exactly," Brooklyn interrupted, with a smirk on her face as if to say, "See? I told you there's nothing to worry about."

Vanessa got the courage to chime in. "Well, yesterday morning, as I walked into class, John texted me. I didn't tell anyone. How did he get my number? Plus, it was from a blocked number. I bet no one here has heard about blocking a number in a text!"

Everyone paused and looked at Vanessa in disbelief. There was a collective moment of doubt that took everyone by surprise.

"Let me see the text!" Jason demanded.

"I don't have my phone. I took it out in Ms. Washington's class and she took it and gave it to Vice Principal Williams."

"Ms. Washington is no joke," interjected Harlem.

"When I get my phone on Monday, I'll show you guys."

"That's not crazy, Vanessa. There's probably plenty of apps that can do that. But, I get you not wanting 'strangers' texting you," Harlem said.

"No one knows this John," Vanessa responded aggressively. "We don't even have a picture of him. His chatroom icon was the artwork of Drake's last album."

"That cover art was sick! But I feel you. We should know what he looks like, especially since no one's met him. Where's he from?" Harlem continued.

"I bet no one knows!" Vanessa snapped. "Everyone is just hyped over pics of his house and his sense of humor."

"Well, I see your point, Vanessa," Harlem said. "There's a lot of trolling online, but you don't really have enough to say, without a doubt, that he's some 'stranger danger' dude. But that's just my opinion. Some girls like being pursued, and others might think what he's doing is creep mode. I would suggest you keep an eye on his Link chat behavior. Better safe than sorry. We have to look out for each other. On that note, later guys! I'm heading over to Sneaker Heaven, looking to get those re-released BRED 11's. My cousin works there…"

Harlem winked at his friends, "…didn't have to spend the night in the line."

"Later," a couple of the kids responded to Harlem. They all exchanged signature handshakes or hugs with him.

"I'll catch up with y'all later, maybe in the Link—so I can take a look at this dude's posts." And with that, he merrily headed off.

"See? Harlem has a point," Justin commented to the remaining friends.

"Yeah, he does," Brooklyn added, "and the point is, Vanessa thinks everyone likes her and she's just overreacting."

"No," Jason chipped in. "We have to keep an eye on this new guy and see if there's any suspicious posts. That's what Harlem was basically saying."

"First, we have to start with asking him to share a pic of himself. Who wants to do that?" asked Justin.

"I'll do it," Vanessa volunteered. "He pays attention to my posts, so he's likely to answer me the fastest," she said, looking at Brooklyn with a sly grin. "Only thing is, I'm faded. I won't have internet access until Monday."

"We can hit up the Internet Café right quick, you can log in and I can grab a caramel frap," suggested Bobby.

"Let's do it!" Jason said, leading the charge. They looked for a free station and pulled out their devices. Vanessa logged in and started a chat. She looked for John and noticed he wasn't online. Everyone else logged in and waited for John to respond, too.

Vanessa began right away with a theory. "I bet this John is not our age. He probably has a real job during the week, and he's out with his kids today. Matter of fact, that dude could be John," Vanessa implicated, pointing to a middle-aged man holding what appeared to be his granddaughter's hand.

Bobby shook his head in disbelief, Brooklyn rolled her eyes, and Justin just pondered it like, "That could be the case." While they waited, they kicked around some ideas on how they could find out if he was a fraud.

"Ask him to meet us to go to the movies," Bobby suggested.

"Better yet, invite him to the pep rally!" Brooklyn offered. It was a tradition the school looked forward to every year.

"Let's focus on getting a picture first and then see if we can confirm his identity," Justin chimed in, always the voice of reason. "One step at a time, guys. This is not a top secret mission."

"Tell that to your bae," Brooklyn yammered, gesturing towards Vanessa. "You guys are acting like John is a master criminal when he's been nothing but cool to everyone."

Frustrated that John was not logged on and tired of her friends' opinions, Vanessa logged off and announced, "I'm going home. I'll catch up with you guys another time." She got up and left the cafe before anyone could stop her.

Justin returned to the table with a smoothie for both him and V to find out that she was gone. Brooklyn grabbed it and said with a grin, "So sweet of you."

Halfway home, Vanessa realized she had missed an opportunity to speak with Justin about Giselle, something that would have made the trip to the mall somewhat productive.

1. Do you think you have good instincts about people? Is your first impression usually right?

_____

_____

_____

2. Explain a situation when you were right or wrong about your first impression.

_____

_____

_____

3. Are you someone that values the opinions of your friends over your own opinions? If so, when has that benefited you? When has it hurt you?

_____

_____

_____

#ADVICE

As soon as Vanessa walked through the door, her mom asked, "How was the mall?"

"Great, just fantastic," she responded robotically. Meanwhile, what she really thought was, *What a waste of time!*

Vanessa went directly to her room to relax for a few and then she planned to call Justin. However, she immediately realized that without access to her phone there was no way to call him. She barely remembered her own home phone number and was shocked that she had remembered Brooklyn's earlier. She definitely didn't know Justin's number by heart. Vanessa went back downstairs.

"Mom, can I just check my cellphone for a number?"

"Sure."

Vanessa grabbed her phone, used the thumbprint to unlock it, and searched for the number. She wrote down Justin's number, but before she passed the phone back to her mom, she noticed she had countless "likes" on IG in her push notifications. There were far too many to wrap her mind around, which was especially puzzling because she hadn't posted anything in a while. Additionally, she had a bunch of text messages. She figured they must be from her friends looking for her last night since she wasn't in the Link.

She held onto the phone another second and took a quick glimpse. To her disbelief, they were all from John—all the "likes" and the texts. Stunned (and totally upset), she locked her phone and gave it back to her mother. She went to the house phone and quickly called Justin.

"Who's this?" Justin answered suspiciously since the number was not familiar to him.

"It's Vanessa. I'm in digital prison, remember? I had to call from the home phone."

"Oh, I almost didn't pick up since I didn't recognize the number. What's up?"

"I wanted to speak to you about Giselle. We've been missing each other and every time I try to get the details, something happens. Finally, I can talk now."

"Well, actually I'm about to head into the movie theater with my mom. It's family fun night. Sorry, can I call you back after the movie?"

"Sure, call this number. Remember, I don't have my cell."

"OK, talk to ya later," Justin replied.

Vanessa went into the kitchen where her mom was making a snack. "Hey, Mom, can I ask you a question?"

"Sure! Anything." Vanessa's mom loved talking to her. Mrs. James was kind of the neighborhood mom. Many of Vanessa's friends confided in her. She took great delight in having the trust of many young ladies in the neighborhood.

They both grabbed a seat at the kitchen counter and Vanessa began to share while grabbing a potato chip off her mother's plate. "I have a friend and she told me that a particular guy is making her feel uncomfortable."

Her mom peered at her, fully engaged, shaking her head in agreement. Vanessa continued, "He pays tons of attention to her online, and I just found out he's now following her on IG. He DMs me, and I, I mean *her*, and she didn't give him her number. None of my friends, I mean (shaking her head for clarity), *her* friends know him, know where he lives, what he looks like, or anything. Sooo, whatcha think?"

"You, I mean your friend, should tell this person that she is not interested in being directly contacted and that he should respect that. I would suggest you block, I mean tell your friend to block his number. Also, if he's on Link, tell your friend not to enter that app. Or, leave the app when he says anything your friend is uncomfortable with. I think he'll get the hint. Then, if he still contacts 'your friend,' I would suggest you tell her to speak with her parents. That's what I think. Do you think your friend will see that as good advice?"

"I think so. Thanks." Meanwhile, different thoughts were looping through Vanessa's mind about who John could really be. It was getting late and she was doubtful whether Justin would call back. Just at that moment, however, the house phone rang. Vanessa raced to pick it up before her nosey little brother answered. But, he got there first.

"Hello, who's this? (Pause.) What do you want with her? (Pause.) You like her? Does she like you? Why don't you come over for dinner sometime?" Riley thought he was being hilarious. Vanessa did not.

She felt very embarrassed and was trying desperately to get the phone away from her brother. Finally, her strength won over. She grabbed the receiver. "Hello?"

"Hey, Vanessa. Your brother is funny." It was Justin on the phone.

"I don't find him funny at all. Anyway, what's up? Can you tell me the story now?"

"I can try, but I'm just leaving the movie theater and I really don't want her listening to our conversation, which will lead to her asking questions and then a conversation with her, you know?"

"It's alright. Just call me when you get home and can talk."

"OK, should be about 20 minutes."

Vanessa sat by the phone and burned with anticipation. Fifteen minutes later, the phone rang and Vanessa picked up immediately. "Justin?"

"No, this is not Justin. Hi, Vanessa. This is Mrs. Walters. Is your mom home?" Mrs. Walters was Riley's best friend's mother.

"Yep, sorry. Hold on, let me get her." Vanessa cupped the receiver with her hand. "Mom!" she yelled at the top of her lungs. "The phone!"

Vanessa's mom took the phone from her. "Thank you, sweetheart."

"Hey, Marie, how are you?"

Vanessa went to her room. She knew that by the time her mother got off the phone with Mrs. Walters, there was no way Justin would think it was OK to call the house. *Ugh!* Vanessa simply went to bed.

When she woke up, it was Sunday morning, and the family was getting ready for church. Vanessa joined them for breakfast. "Mom, did I get any calls last night?"

"As a matter of fact, you did," Mom responded as she sipped her fruit smoothie. "John called."

Vanessa started choking on her toast. It was an involuntary reaction. After coughing and catching her breath, she asked her mother again. "Who called?"

"John," her mother repeated. "He sounded very mature and polite."

"Is his number on the caller ID?" Vanessa inquired with a sense of urgency.

"No, it was a blocked number. I only answered because Dad wasn't home, and, you know, we always pick up when one of us are out, just to be sure it's not an emergency."

Vanessa could not believe this guy. He had direct messaged her and now he had called her house. Very frustrated at this point, she couldn't wait to get to youth group to let everyone know what had happened—and to catch up with Justin to get the details on what she was certain would link John and Giselle.

HOW ABOUT YOU?

1. What adult do you feel comfortable talking to? Why?

_____

_____

_____

2. What stops you from telling adults your problems?

_____

_____

_____

3. When you get advice from an adult, how does it make you feel?

_____

_____

_____

7

#FINALLY

After youth group, Vanessa was able to speak to Justin alone. She shared that last night John had called, but that she didn't actually talk to him. They both stared at each other in utter disbelief. "This is something to be concerned about," Justin said very seriously.

"You're telling me?" Vanessa responded ironically. She motioned to Justin to continue with the story.

"Oh, yeah. Giselle went to West Side High and the story went that she met some guy in a cheer squad Link. He was funny, cool, and everyone liked him. He started pinging her DM from time to time, liked her posts, and followed all her social media accounts. I heard she was impressed with him but that she didn't really know who he was. I guess she followed him because her friends followed him. Rumor had it that his father was a professional athlete and that was the reason for the pics of his house. The pics always made people want to be cool with him. That's what Nate told me."

Out of nowhere, Vanessa blurted, "Is Giselle dead?"

Surprised at her question, Justin responded with deep concern on his face. "No, she's alive, but she moved right after this happened."

"OK, go ahead, what next?"

"I was told that they texted each other for weeks and that he kept asking her out, but she said that they should hang out as a group until she got to know him."

"Smart. I like that. Good idea," Vanessa added.

"I heard that he said he wasn't into that. He told Giselle that because of his father's fame, he didn't like being in crowds and that people always tried to use him for his parents' money. He would always 'like' her photos on the 'Gram and even gave her tips on how to get more followers. He was always complimenting her and writing nice things in her comments. No one really thought to ask around about this guy."

"What was his name?" asked Vanessa.

"I think Nate told me his name was Jay, but I'm not sure. Anyway, since Giselle was on the cheerleading team, all her friends thought this type of attention was normal. She was very outgoing and friendly. No one worried that anything was wrong with Jay. He was popular online. After Giselle moved, everyone realized that no one actually knew him."

Vanessa was shaking her head with a contemptuous look as if to say, "This is exactly what is happening now and no one sees it that way!"

Justin continued, "While all this was going on, they just liked his pics and the lifestyle he promoted online, and so no one cared if it was real or not. That didn't seem to cross anyone's mind. He had tons of followers, but when the police looked into his account, they were fake followers. He bought them. He paid for followers. Apparently, that's a thing now."

Vanessa was busy putting the pieces together in her head, one of them being that she, too, was on the cheer squad—and tried to connect any other similarities. "Insane. What else?"

"Nate told me that one night, Jay was able to convince Giselle to let him visit her while her parents were working late that night."

"That's crazy! I can't have company when my parents aren't home. And to invite someone from online I've never met before? No way!" she said, shaking her head in disapproval.

"That's what everyone says, V. We know some things are wrong, and we still do them," Justin said, admitting to poor judgment from time to time. "We shouldn't be in a hurry to judge her. You never know what you'll do or not do in the heat of the moment."

Pausing to reflect on the wisdom bomb Justin had just dropped, Vanessa nodded her head in agreement. "True," she responded. "I guess you're right. It just sounds so far out there to me, but you're right. What happened next?"

"Well, after she agreed to let him come to her house, she called a friend of hers to let her know. Just in case something happened. So, her friend came over and hid in another room—just to have her back."

"That's super smart!"

"Yeah, I thought so, too," replied Justin.

"Then?"

"Well, he pinged her that he was uncomfortable coming over because her parents could come home at any time and he said he didn't want her to get into trouble. He also said that his father went away for a game and that his mother was away on business. So instead, they arranged to meet at his house. However, he gave her an address that was not an actual home address. When he gave her the address, Giselle searched online maps for it, and the aerial view appeared to be some random warehouse, in an area she was not familiar with. Either way, it certainly wasn't a house or anywhere the son of a professional athlete would live. That, she knew. So, when she shared that info with Jay, he replied that he must have given her the wrong address by mistake, and then agreed to come over to her house."

"See? That would have made me think something was definitely off."

"Maybe. But, you don't know till you're in it. I read that about one in 20 kids arrange secret meetings with someone they meet online. Plus, how many times do we do something that feels wrong just to look cool or be accepted? I mean, look, it happened to me. I bought these Nike Airs for way more money than I could afford. I had to save up for months. And for what? Just to impress a girl that didn't even notice

I got them? By the time I got them, they just released a new pair, limited editions, with even crazy better colors."

Shrugging, as to indicate "not a great example, dude," Vanessa went on to say, "Well, if a girl only notices you because of new kicks, she's pretty shallow and probably not the type you'd want to be with anyway. Who was this? Carmen?"

Justin ignored Vanessa's inquiry and continued, "I guess. But it's not like that in school. Everything is about popularity. I don't feel like I can just be myself sometimes. It's stressful. I bet Giselle just enjoyed the attention."

Vanessa was shocked to hear him say that. To her, Justin was one of the most grounded, friendly, respected, smartest dudes she knew.

Continuing, he added, "Why else would she feel pressured to meet a stranger that no one knew?"

"She was already on the cheerleading squad and had plenty of friends. Looking from the outside, Giselle seemed to have it all, Justin."

"I agree, but being popular on social media is a big deal to our friends."

"I notice that you don't have an IG account," Vanessa stated curiously.

"Yeah, I closed it. I never told anyone the truth when they asked why I closed it. I just tell people I'm too busy to be on social media. But the truth is, I once posted a pic of my new sneakers, and Kevin…"

"The football team captain?" Vanessa interrupted for clarity.

"Yeah, that Kevin. Well, he made a comment about my post and faded me. I still remember what he posted in the comments. 'Those were hot three summers ago. But no one wears those anymore.' And then he added a thumbs down." Justin showed Vanessa a screenshot of the post.

"Wow, that's not cool. And you knew Kevin! Didn't you tutor him in math? If it weren't for you, he wouldn't even have been on the team this season. He thinks he's all that because he plays football," Vanessa said, shaking her head with revulsion. "That's pretty lame!"

"Yeah, but no one disagreed with him. I felt like crap."

"Well, if it means anything, I didn't see the comment. And if I had seen it, I would *not* have 'liked' it."

"What you may or may not realize is that people that I am cool with liked it. I'm talking about friends that I would have never thought faded me. It's strange. It's like, when people are online, they change. They post stuff they normally wouldn't say, and even show pics and videos that are inappropriate. They act out of character."

Vanessa listened intently as Justin went on. "They smile in your face and fade you online. I just got tired of it. I've seen videos of fights, too. I remember back in the day, if you were having a fight, your friends would try to break it up so you didn't get hurt. Now they grab their phone so they can record and post it ASAP. I have bigger plans and better things to do than defend my life's decisions online. My G-Pa always told me that you should treat people the way you want to be treated. The deal is, my dad is not around, and my mom can't afford to buy me the newest stuff—and I don't want to feel bad on social media because I'm not making my life 'look' perfect. I'm off that!"

Justin looked resolute making his point. Vanessa looked at Justin with a renewed admiration for her friend. Her brain was also taking in everything he was saying; she was beginning to form a new opinion about social media.

Justin continued, "I never told anyone this, so please keep it on the low. Kevin's parents got a divorce last summer and since then, he hasn't been the same. I already forgave him, even though he never apologized, because I know he's dealing with stuff. His dad used to be at every practice and every game. Now…nothing. Kevin's been taking his pain out on others and doesn't even know it. To him, it's all jokes."

Vanessa conjectured, "I feel you. I wonder if that's why Brooklyn is so quick to dis me sometimes. Her life at home isn't always the greatest. Thankfully, my mom's been reaching out to her."

"Probably," Justin reacted with understanding. "Plus, she's new to the group and we all grew up together. That's gotta make her feel like an outsider sometimes. As for Kevin, he probably thought he was soooo funny when he posted that. He talks to me all the time like nothing ever happened."

"That's sad," Vanessa interjected, continuing to listen.

"Dealing with online drama, from people that you thought were friends, is too much for me to bother with social media—at least right now, anyway. When I used to go on, I would get tired of being notified about what this person ate, who they were with, and how great of a time they were having 24/7. Some kids just be doing too much. They be on

OD mode. But when I see them in the hallway or in class, their real life ain't looking so great. Their grades are chump, and they don't look like they're going anywhere, real fast. That's that filter life right there. Hey, that's just me, Vanessa."

"I gotcha, Jus. It's a lot. We deal with stuff every day. Does this person like me today and not tomorrow? Why did this person post that mean message about such a private matter? It just happens…" Vanessa was in deep thought.

"…but I also feel like social media is a way to keep in touch. Voice your opinion. Create awareness, spread a message, and find out what's going on. But then there's the other side. It's used to hurt people, sometimes by mistake and sometimes on purpose. Females do things that make no sense at times. They don't know they're getting a tattoo."

"Tattoo?" Justin asked, totally confused. "Vanessa, what are you talking about?"

"A digital tattoo. The stuff you post never ever, ever, ever disappears. It stays in cyberspace, in the cloud." They both looked up and laughed.

"You're smart, Justin. You don't think that once you press delete, it actually deletes, do you?" He looked slightly confused. "Of course you knew that. Right? Right?"

Justin nodded his head as if to say he was fully aware of this. He wasn't willing to admit that he was clueless, and that was the first he had heard about a digital tattoo.

HOW ABOUT YOU?

1. Have you ever mistakenly posted private information about someone? What was the outcome?

_____

_____

_____

2. Has anyone ever posted private information about you? If so, how did it make you feel?

_____

_____

_____

3. If you saw a post like Kevin's that was rude to your friend, do you think you would have the courage to respond to Kevin to protect and support your friend?

_____

_____

_____

4. When was the last time someone was hurtful and you felt alone because no one came to your defense?

_____

_____

_____

5. How has your social media experience been so far? On a scale of 1-10, 10 being great, rate your experience. Why?

_____

_____

_____

6. Do you see social media as a positive or negative tool to communicate? Why?

_____

_____

_____

8

#T.H.I.N.K.

"Justin, my cousin is in college and she went for an internship at Snap. And because some pics her ex posted of her were found online, they took back the opportunity," Vanessa explained with intensity.

"Took back? What do you mean?"

"She went through the interviews, and they said if the background check comes back good, she's in. References? Check. Criminal history? Check. Drug test? Check. But once it got to the background check…" Vanessa imitated the "slit throat" gesture.

"Wow, it wasn't even her fault," Justin said in shock. "So she lost the internship? They didn't care that she didn't post them?"

"Naw. Companies care about your judgment. We do stuff in the heat of the moment like life's carefree and it's all good. But, every day is 'decision day', my dude. She didn't post the pics, but she took them and sent them to her ex when they were dating. You feel me? She sent them! That was not a wise decision. Once you press 'send', what someone does with it afterwards is no longer in your control. Apparently, when they broke up, he thought it was a good idea to put them online. When Snap found them, they told her it was a no go. It got crazy. Her brother found out and the families got involved. It was insane."

"Wow, digital tattoo. I wonder what's my digital tattoo," Justin responded with curiosity.

"All the companies are checking social media posts. They want to know who you really are when you're not at work. Imagine if you get a job with First Sports, your dream job in sports broadcasting. Say you're the next Chris Broussard and covering the NBA, and you're hosting shows and just living the dream. Then, out of nowhere, a pic of you surfaces and the report is, 'NBA insider from blah, blah, blah fired!' If you embarrass the company, they will fire you. It's that serious. We're young and we don't think about this stuff, but that opened my eyes to my digital tattoo and how it can affect my future. That's why I am easy online. And plus, my parents don't play that. You don't see me in pics that are questionable. It's a small world. What we do today affects tomorrow. Real talk! My father is not a big fan of social media, but he sees the benefits and knows how it's a big part of how people communicate today. He just reminds me to T.H.I.N.K. before I post. Is what I'm going to post True? Is it Helpful? Is it Inspiring? Is it Necessary? And is it Kind? He says if it passes the T.H.I.N.K. test, go for it."

Justin listened and looked at Vanessa with the same look of admiration she had given him just moments earlier. Then, he responded, "The T.H.I.N.K. test, nice, I like it. That's unfortunate what happened to your cousin, though."

"Anyway, we were talking about Giselle. When she found out the address was a warehouse and he decided to go over to her house instead, what happened next?"

Just then, Vanessa's father walked over. "Vanessa, we've got to get going. We have a couple of errands to run before we get home." Her conversation with Justin was abruptly ended. Again.

"I'll call you later, Justin."

"Later, Vanessa. Have a nice day, Mr. James." Vanessa shot a nod back to Justin as she and her family headed off.

1. Do you know your digital tattoo?

_____

_____

_____

2. If you went for your dream job, do you think everything would be okay with the posts you've made?

_____

_____

_____

3. What's one post that you wish you could take back?

_____

_____

_____

4. Why did you post it in the first place? What do you think was wrong with it as you deeply think about it now?

_____

_____

_____

9

#ITHAPPENS

After running errands and doing her chores, Vanessa got so distracted (and tired) that she forgot to call Justin. Vanessa woke up bright and early Monday morning, feeling really good. She hated to admit it, but not having her phone throughout the weekend allowed her more rest. She was getting her phone back today and that excited her, too. Eager to see what she had missed, she raced downstairs to her mom.

Vanessa praised her mom—just before asking for her laptop, cellphone, and tablet back. "Mom, I understand my punishment, and I respect you guys and the rules. Thank you for loving me and disciplining me. I really appreciate the safe environment and boundaries you guys set up for me."

Vanessa's post-punishment speech upset Riley every time. He could never tell if she was being sincere. But most importantly, it made him jealous. He knew how much their parents loved it when his sister said those things, yet Riley still couldn't bring himself to say them.

She wolfed down breakfast, grabbed her cellphone, and looked at Dad. "I know, I won't take it out in class." Dad froze with his mouth open, just about to say the exact same thing. Vanessa gave her parents a hug and kiss, love-slapped Riley in the back of his head, and was off.

The school bus came a little early that morning and she moved a little faster to catch up. Strolling to a seat on the bus, head down, powering on her cell, she greeted her classmates and focused on her unanswered text messages. Vanessa grabbed a seat next to Brooklyn. Brooklyn looked happy to see her friend.

"Welcome back, V. We missed you in the chatroom. And guess who wasn't asking for you?"

"Who?" Vanessa asked, knowing the answer already.

"John, yep, he was online, cracking jokes, being his normal cool self. He shared some sites where we can download music and movies for free."

"Good for you guys. I'm glad he wasn't asking for me." Brooklyn smirked at Vanessa's comment, not really believing her. Brooklyn was convinced Vanessa loved attention.

With her head in her phone, Vanessa continued, "Like I keep saying, no one knows John, and I don't think he is who he says he is anyway. Justin was telling me more about the Giselle…"

"Oh, that story from Big Nate?" Brooklyn interrupted. "Whatever. I don't believe that just because one bad thing happened across town, it's going to happen to me, you, or any one of us."

"Hey, you feel the way you feel, that's on you. Obviously, you like John. You can have him. Just be careful," Vanessa warned.

"I don't need your permission to get up with John. He's moved on from you and started texting me. I just wanted to tell you first so there's no shade later when you come back to the chat and he's not focused on you."

"Perfect," Vanessa said sincerely.

"Perfect!" Brooklyn triumphantly responded.

Both girls continued focusing on their phones and adjusted their earbuds, using music to drown out the conversation neither of them wanted to continue.

To Vanessa's surprise (and satisfaction), she didn't have any more texts from John, or whatever his real name was. With a sigh of relief, she thought, *I'm glad he got the hint and dipped off.*

Vanessa was still curious about John in the sense that his identity was still unconfirmed. And although she and Brooklyn were not "besties" at this very moment, she cared about her friends safety. The more Vanessa learned about trolling, online pervs, and the "hype life" (her new term for people who only share how great their lives are), the more she developed a different mindset for social media.

Vanessa deliberated with herself. *Convincing Brooklyn to be careful is going to be a challenge. I'm sure she's just going to assume that I'm blocking.*

Fortunately, the day went by without incident and after homework and dinner, Vanessa logged in to the Link. Everyone was there. Jason was the host. Jokes and funny pics were posted, and Harlem was asking the group who was planning on spending the night waiting in line for Summer Jam XX tickets. It was coming to the arena, and it was the annual, mega hip-hop concert promoted by the #1 radio station in the city.

"There's no way my mom is letting me camp out overnight," responded Justin out of nowhere.

Then, Brooklyn posted, "Oh, look who's here. 😲 This must be a special occasion! Justin has taken time from his busy schedule."

"What's up, Jus?" several friends typed.

"What's up?" a few others posted. Justin totally ignored Brooklyn's sarcastic remark.

Vanessa, without delay, asked John to post a picture of himself. She had not forgotten the plan they agreed to. The room went silent. Everyone pretty much knew how Vanessa and Justin felt, especially since the Giselle story. No one typed a chat for what seemed like hours. After about fifteen seconds, John responded.

"Cool, I have a pic from this weekend's party at the PAL. DJ did the music. It was crazy!" And ping, just like that, John shared what he claimed to be a picture of himself.

"Which one are you?" Vanessa asked, not planning to relent until she felt comfortable.

"Fall back," Brooklyn responded immediately. "He shared a pic. What are you trying to do? 😠 Get off his back about it."

"Why so salty, Brooklyn? I can ask what I want. Stay in your lane. It's a party photo with lots of people in it, even some adults. And whoever took the pic shouldn't consider a career in photography. If I was in the same room with John right now, I still wouldn't know who he was. 😵 I'm just saying."

Nothing but silence ensued. Then ping. "I'm the one second from the left."

Brooklyn posted 😊 and everyone started chatting again .

"What school do you attend, John?" Vanessa continued, followed instantly by 😦 posted by Brooklyn.

"I go to Hillside Academy for the Gifted and Talented. It's a private school."

Vanessa was disappointed that she didn't know anyone there that could confirm John's identity. The rest of the crew seemed sold and happy with John's responses. Vanessa was certain Brooklyn was okay with his answers, too, especially since she had defended him and has had no doubts about him in the first place.

Brooklyn was happy that John was able to convince everyone else with his answers. *Now nobody will see him as a threat to the group* was Brooklyn's thinking. With all the shared "hype life" photos, she was definitely digging on John.

Vanessa phoned Justin directly, so they could talk outside the Link. "Well, you read it. Whatcha think? Does he seem for real?" Justin asked.

"He does," Vanessa responded, "but why do I still feel like he's a creep?"

"I don't know, but let me finish telling you about Giselle. Where did we leave off?"

"You were saying how the dude gave her a weird address then decided to come to her house, something like that."

"Oh yeah, that's it. So, he decided to come to her house. I heard the girls were like setting up where one of her friends would hide, and if anything happened, she'd make sure she was ready to call the police."

"I like this girl, Justin. She's smart, and she planned it out. Not like Brooklyn. I'm concerned for her."

Justin continued with the story. "Just wait… So, the dude came in and was able to make Giselle feel really comfortable. He was actually much older than he said—he just had a baby face. They talked for a while and he asked if anyone was in the house. Feeling comfortable and very impressed that such a mature dude would be interested in her, she said she had a friend in the house and called her down. Her friend Aubrey came down and met Jay. Just then, Jay abruptly asked to use the bathroom."

Vanessa was enthralled in the story and dared not interrupt.

"Nate told me that what happened next is stuff you only see in the movies. He couldn't believe it himself. Jay evidently had friends that were outside in a van. He texted them when he'd gone into the bathroom. Jay went back to the living room to hang with Giselle. About five minutes later, the doorbell rang. Giselle wondered aloud who that could be. Jay said it was pizza, that he thought he would surprise her.

"Giselle seemed excited that Jay seemed to be as thoughtful as he was cute. Aubrey smiled and opened the door without asking who it was. To her surprise, two guys stormed in and pushed her to the floor, knocking her unconscious as her head crashed into the coffee table. One guy grabbed Giselle by the throat with one hand and placed his other over her mouth to subdue her and muffle any attempt for her to yell for help."

Vanessa gasped in disbelief and shock.

Justin continued, "Fortunately for the girls, a car pulled into the driveway at that very instant. As the headlights peered through the living room windows, it startled Jay and his thugs. They immediately ran off. They exited through the side door and ran up the block, where their van was parked. You could tell they had scoped out the house prior to that night. They knew how to keep the van out of sight so it wouldn't draw attention from neighbors. It just happened that Giselle's father came home early because he didn't feel well."

"I, I...can't even imagine..." Vanessa stuttered.

"As soon as Giselle's dad arrived, he noticed the door was ajar. As he entered, he saw his daughter crying, rubbing her neck, and trying to catch her breath. Then, he spotted Aubrey on the floor, unconscious, with blood dripping from her head. He was stricken with disbelief, and Giselle was in an uncontrollable state of hysteria."

Vanessa couldn't register what she was hearing. Her initial response was, "No, you can't be serious. You made this up. You believe this Nate dude? Are you serious?"

"I'm serious. Nate's father is a cop. He knows everything that goes down," Justin responded, justifying his claims.

"This is crazy! What were they going to do to them? Do you know?" Vanessa inquired.

"Kidnap them and take them somewhere. It was a big deal. The cops are always trying to educate us about strange people on the internet. Now I get why. Remember that community police officer that came to school last year to talk about cyber-bullying and online safety? That was Nate's dad."

Vanessa nodded, remembering the assembly Justin was referring to. *Too bad so many of us weren't paying attention.*

"Right? Anyway, Giselle was so scared, her family had to move. She was freaked out from the incident, but she became completely traumatized when the police told her what could have potentially happened if her dad didn't come home when he did. I am talking kidnapping, and all the horror that comes with it—forced drugs, sex, and even slavery. These are things we see on the news. For some reason, we don't think these things can ever happen to us."

"We've got to warn Brooklyn!" Vanessa said with concern and conviction.

"I'm with you. She's going to have to believe us when we tell her this story."

Thinking about Brooklyn's personality, Vanessa countered, "Well, she doesn't have to believe us. Let's at least hope she trusts us. I think you should tell her, Justin. She'll think I don't want her to be happy. For some reason, she thinks I have a problem with her."

"Okay, I can do that. Hey, instead, why don't we *both* tell her tomorrow at school with our guidance counselor, Mr. Jones?" Justin suggested.

"That's a great idea," Vanessa remarked, offering a fist bump to Justin. "I think that will work!"

1. Have you ever tried to meet someone from social media in person?

   _____

   _____

   _____

2. Do you have any friends that meet people from social media in person?

   _____

   _____

   _____

3. Did you know that fraudulent internet meetings happen every day all over the country?

   _____

   _____

   _____

4. Do you think what happened to Giselle and Aubrey could happen to you or someone you know?

   _____

   _____

   _____

10

#SQUADGOALS

First thing the next morning, Vanessa and Justin met in front of their guidance counselor's office. They spoke to Mr. Jones about their concerns for Brooklyn's safety.

"I understand what you're saying..." Mr. Jones had heard about Giselle. But he reminded Vanessa and Justin that he was the one who had arranged the assembly with the community police officer. He also reminded them that a majority of the students didn't take the subject or the officer's warnings seriously.

"And I understand all that," Vanessa respectfully responded, "but this really happened, and we want to warn our friend. But we believe that she won't listen to us. We need you to set up the meeting."

Mr. Jones asked for the details, and then shared his outlook on the situation. "Guys, I hear that you want to protect your friend, but there's just not enough to go on right now. Is this John harassing her or making her feel uncomfortable in any way? Has he asked for money or any other odd favors or requests? You asked for a picture, and he gave it. You asked where he went to school, and he told you. Right now, it sounds like you could be mistaken about John, and maybe, just maybe, the unfortunate incident with Giselle was an isolated event and won't happen again around here."

"It's not just *that* Mr. Jones. He called my home phone number, and direct messaged me, and I never gave him either number. He just seems creepy."

"Well, if I search your name online, there's a good chance I can get your home number, address, cellphone number, social security number, probably your class schedule, and blood type. That information is online; these are the times we live in. When I was a kid..."

Vanessa and Justin looked at each other as if to say, "Ugh, not another Jones-ism." (Mr. Jones was known for his stories. They made a point, but it took a while to get there.)

"Sorry, Mr. Jones, I just realized I have a test first period. I should go."

"Yeah, I have a presentation," Vanessa added. "I gotta go, too."

They both jumped out of their seats and left Mr. Jones in mid-sentence. As they walked to class, Justin commented, "He's right. Right now, our evidence of John being a bad dude is slim. We really don't have much to go on. Maybe we're over-thinking it."

"Maybe." Vanessa shrugged and headed for her first class.

It was school-as-usual the rest of the morning. Uneventful, until lunch. There always seemed to be drama in the cafeteria.

Much of the Monday melodrama was from weekend social-media drama. Usually, the girls were upset with each other for not "liking" their posts or someone had written something mean or insensitive. They usually would make up by Wednesday, and by Friday, they'd be besties again. Then, the cycle would repeat itself, and it would be a circus again the following Monday.

Standing outside of the cafeteria, Vanessa was talking to Justin. "I never really understood why getting 'likes' was so important until I started posting. It's intense, I mean, to post a picture of yourself and not one of your friends compliment you. Ouch, that kinda hurts," Vanessa said with a face as if she just swallowed a lemon.

"My feelings were crushed the first time I posted. I didn't get any likes. Can you imagine that, Jus?" she said, conveying a bit of depression. "I felt a way. I would check back every 10 minutes, refresh my screen, and be like, *This is not cool.*

"Later, I realized that my privacy settings were on, and no one actually saw my post. I felt kinda embarrassed for myself. When I fixed the problem and turned off my privacy settings, I started to get positive feedback. But to be honest, thinking back, I don't like the power it had over me. Apparently, subconsciously, I needed the approval of people..."

Justin, shaking his head, interrupted to say, "Psychology class got you reflecting, huh?"

Vanessa peered at Justin with a smirk. "Yeah, it was something that I never thought I would feel. It was a wakeup call. Thankfully, I got clued in on my first post. Some people post all day. They share anything and everything they're doing. And if they don't get enough likes, they delete the post or get mad at their online friends for not liking, commenting, or sharing. It causes tons of resentment, disappointment, self-doubt, and low self-esteem. I've seen the coolest girls post very risky pics. I know them. And I feel bad that they post stuff that they *think* is no big deal."

"Digital tattoo," they both said in unison, nodding in agreement.

"They're not thinking, really. They don't realize the long-term effects," Vanessa continued. "If someone they know wants to be mean, they can take a screenshot of the pic, add some nasty words to it, and then repost it."

"Meme!" they said in unison again as they both busted out laughing.

"Most times, you won't even know who did it. The pic just stays out there. What a terrible feeling! Anyone can take that pic and keep reposting to different sites. Next thing you know, you're online looking cray-cray. That's not a nice place to be."

Vanessa continued, with Justin nodding in agreement. "It's the worst. Every lunch table you sit at, someone is complaining about a post. As if I don't have anything else to worry about like grades, chores, and today's game against our cross-town rivals? This is the biggest volleyball game of the season. Both teams qualified for the Nationals

Tournament by winning our bracket. We are undefeated and they are undefeated. Coach's been stressing the importance of this game because the winner receives a scholarship to a premier volleyball camp. Everyone that goes to this camp and performs well will be handpicked for a D-1 scholarship. I know my parents would love for me to go."

"You got this, Vanessa. You guys are ranked number one for a reason."

"Thanks, Jus." She gave him a sincere look of appreciation. "I'll meet you at the lunch table. I'm going to drop off my books at my locker."

She began walking down the hallway and spotted Brooklyn a few feet away. Out of character, Vanessa shouted, "Hey! How's your chatroom bae that no one has ever met?"

In character, Brooklyn yelled back, "You jealous that John is showing interest in *me* now?"

When Vanessa got to her locker, she texted Brooklyn. "Trust me. I hope this John guy turns out to be as nice in person as he is in the Link."

Brooklyn responded, "Sure, V, I bet. 😒 You expect me to believe that you support me in this?" Brooklyn's eyes were looking down at her phone for a response. But Vanessa was now standing behind Brooklyn, peering over her left shoulder. Brooklyn startled slightly, and both girls smiled at each other. Vanessa continued the conversation in person.

"I support you being safe first, and then happy. That's my main concern. I'd rather you be mad at me for caring instead of liking me and not sure if I got your back."

"Ah, you're so sweet," Brooklyn said with an obvious hint of sarcasm as she grabbed her lunch out of her locker and headed to the cafeteria with Vanessa trailing, seemingly still trying to explain herself.

Once Vanessa sat down at the same table as Brooklyn, Brooklyn got up and moved to Samantha's table. Vanessa just shook her head, clearly disappointed that Brooklyn didn't believe her—and disappointed that this whole Link dilemma was causing a rift in their friendship.

Justin walked over to the table. "What's up, Vanessa? What's wrong?"

"Nothing," she responded, clearly lying.

"I saw you talking to Brooklyn and then when I turned around she was at Samantha's table. I know that can't be good. Are you still claiming that something's wrong with John?"

"Yes and no. I was kind of mean and said, 'What's up with your chatroom boyfriend?'"

"Ouch, that can't be nice to hear."

"I know. I'll apologize. I was frustrated and confused. I'm just feeling a lot of pressure from schoolwork, homework, the game, chores, this Giselle thing… There's a lot going on," Vanessa said in a dejected tone.

"Yeah, but as long as we stick together it'll be OK. I got you! If you need something, let me know. Anyway, we just have to respect Brooklyn's space. We don't want to be those annoying friends. Once she feels we're against her, the more she'll pull away—and the more she's going to want to be with John just to prove something to us. Let's act like nothing's wrong, that we're over it, and let's just keep an eye on things from afar."

"I'm on board. Good plan, Jus. We can do that. She's our friend, right or wrong. And in this case, I hope we're wrong. I'll see you later. At the game?"

"For sure. I'll convince Brooklyn to come," Justin replied, to which Vanessa smiled and thought, *that would be nice*, with a tinge of guilt from her earlier comment.

HOW ABOUT YOU?

1. Have you ever had to go against what seemed easy in order to do what's right in a friendship? If so, how?

_____

_____

_____

2. Has being honest helped or hurt your friendship(s)? What's your most memorable example?

_____

_____

_____

3. Do you feel like you can speak to your guidance counselor or a faculty member about serious school and personal concerns?

_____

_____

_____

4. If not, would you try to find an alternate responsible adult to speak to about your concerns or problems? If so, who would that person be? If not, how else do you think you could get help?

_____

_____

_____

11

#THEGAME

The excitement was like nothing Vanessa had ever experienced. Her school hadn't been in the Varsity State finals in 12 years, and Vanessa, being the Comets' team Captain, was having an MVP performance. The match was tied at one set each. Starting set three, Vanessa prepared to serve the volleyball. *This is crazy! It feels like our whole school is here!*

I have to keep it away from Kim, Vanessa told herself. Kim was the Wildcats' best player. Kim was an amazing athlete, an all-star in the state, and as a junior, she already had Division 1 scholarship offers. Kim was always in the local newspaper for her volleyball and track talent. Vanessa looked up to Kim and Kim treated Vanessa like her equal. They had a healthy respect for one another and admired each other's competitiveness and talent.

Vanessa tossed the ball straight up, arched her back to extend her arms, took a leap, and smacked the ball dead-center in the middle of the opponent's front court. The ball strategically landed in between two defenders as both players hesitated to lunge forward in fear of banging into each other.

Both the Wildcats' front-court players looked at each other as if to say, "I thought you had it!" The stakes were high. The winner would be awarded the State Championship

Trophy, bragging rights, and an all-expense paid scholarship to the Elite Summer Volleyball Camp. That was the camp Kim's team had been going to for the last two years as reigning champs.

The crowd went wild. Keisha gave Vanessa a high five and Melissa patted her on the rear end for encouragement. Vanessa looked in the stands at her dad who was celebrating wildly. Vanessa told herself, *We're almost there.*

Coach G. was yelling, "Let's go. Keep it up! Let's close out strong. We got this!" Vanessa gave her a nod and tried to remain cool. She strategically served in the same exact place thinking, *That just might be the soft spot.*

Once again, the toss, the jump, the hit, and out of nowhere, Kim smashed the serve before anyone knew what happened. The crowd went wild, and whatever momentum Vanessa's team just had, just took a quick shift in the opposite direction. Kim was clearly not going down without a fight. That must have been her 10th spike of the match—something she was known for because of her exceptional height and agility. Kim gave a yell in an attempt to get her teammates excited. It worked.

The next three points went to the Wildcats, which made it 7-7, and Coach G. called a time-out. Vanessa immediately addressed the team. "Guys, it's right there. We've come too far as a team not to close this out as champs. So let's refocus. We are the number one seed for a reason. Let's get back to what makes us great. Team work!"

Coach G. nodded as Vanessa's leadership skills went on full display. "All for one, y'all!" Vanessa gestured to her team that they put their hands in for their customary shout, "Teamwork on three. One, two, three... TEAMWORK!"

With that, Justin and Brooklyn started chanting in the stands, "Let's go Comets, Let's go Comets, Let's go Comets!"

With renewed spirit, the team felt energized and inspired. Everyone seemed to get their edge back. They got three of the next five points making it 10-9 in favor of the Comets. Just then, there was an argument at the scorer's table. One of the Wildcats' parents complained to the coach that the score was wrong. This seemed like a lowly attempt to break the Comets' momentum. Nonetheless, the referees had to take a serious look at it.

This break allowed all the players to make substitutions and get a drink of water. Brooklyn and Justin ran down near the Comets' bench. "V, you killing it. Just a couple of more points and we the champs," Brooklyn said hyped and totally into the game.

"Yeah, Vanessa, this game is crazy. Keep it up," Justin added with a fist pump.

"Thanks for coming," Vanessa said, directing her attention to Brooklyn specifically. And then she added, "I'm sorry for the earlier comment. That was chump on my part."

"What comment?" Brooklyn said with a smile, as to indicate, *It's all good.*

Vanessa was visibly happy to see Brooklyn and felt a renewed sense of determination now that her two besties were there. The referees whistled that the score had been confirmed. By the way, that unruly parent who accused the scorekeeper of cheating was removed from the gym. *Weird. I never saw that before,* Vanessa thought as she made her way back towards the court.

Vanessa shouted to her team, "Nothing's changed. We're focused. Now let's get after it!" This is why Vanessa was voted team captain. She wore her heart on her sleeve and was a super motivator.

When the game resumed, the score was still 10-9 in favor of the Comets and it was Cindy's serve. Cindy was a weak server, but she and Vanessa had been working on Cindy's skills outside of practice. Vanessa turned around to give her a wink. "You got this," she mouthed so that only Cindy saw her. The next few points went back and forth until it was game point for the Comets and Jessica was serving for the match. You could hear a pin drop until Jessica's dad yelled, "Let's go, Jess!"

The serve went up, and after an intense volley, Vanessa got the angle, made eye contact with Cindy, went up for the slam off the beautiful pass, and bam! Game Comets! The crowd went wild. But, as Vanessa came down, she landed on Cindy's foot and twisted her ankle. The crowd was too excited to notice Vanessa was in pain. Everyone from the school stormed the court and hoisted Vanessa on their shoulders. Her father noticed something wasn't right by the grimace on his daughter's face. As he made his way to his daughter, she confirmed that she had landed awkwardly. Dad waved over the trainer and they iced her ankle while waiting for the trophy presentation.

Kim made her way over to the Comets' bench and gave Vanessa a hug. "Congratulations. You're going to love the Elite camp. Feel better!"

Vanessa replied humbly, "Thanks, I'll call you. I want to speak to you about something." Little did either girl know that that would be the last time they would speak.

Back home, Mom prepared Vanessa's favorite meal, which was turkey burgers and french fries. Riley made a sign that read, "Welcome Home Champ." It was a great family night— until the doorbell rang. Vanessa's dad signed for it and then announced she had a delivery. He brought the balloons and flowers into the living room, which was met with "oohs" and "aahs" from Mrs. Williams. Vanessa also had a big smile on her face, until she read the unsigned card to herself.

The enclosed note read, "Congratulations on the win and the MVP performance! I hope your ankle feels better. P.S. You can really play. I think you're better than Kim ☺."

Vanessa didn't want to think it, but she did. *No way what's his face sent these!*

1. Do you consider yourself someone that is quick to forgive others? Can you elaborate your forgiveness philosophy?

_____

_____

_____

2. When have you found it impossible (or almost impossible) to forgive a friend's actions?

_____

_____

_____

3. Do you have any friends that you need to forgive, but haven't? If so, who and why?

_____

_____

_____

4. What small step can you take now to repair the relationship?

_____

_____

_____

12

#SOFTMOVE

Brooklyn was already dancing with a red cup in her hand, along with two boys, when Vanessa and Justin arrived. DJ shouted Vanessa's arrival and the crowd momentarily acknowledged her with cheers, waves, and hugs before getting back to whatever they were doing. Vanessa waved some smoke out of her face and gave a cough. Bobby's parents were out of town, so he used this as a perfect reason to throw a party in the name of school spirit, of course. He dubbed it "The Pep-Rally Prequel: Home Edition" and "#pre_pep" on social media for short.

Having just won the championship game after a 6-year drought, Bobby made it seem like he was celebrating the girls' volleyball championship victory until Vanessa noticed that only she and Cindy were invited.

"What's up, girl?" Vanessa shouted over the loud music, pulling Brooklyn out of the boy sandwich she was in.

"Hey, V!" Brooklyn responded, still dancing and smiling from ear to ear. "I'll be right back," she mouthed to the boys she was dancing with (who happened to be two upperclassmen football players).

Vanessa pulled Brooklyn in close so that she could hear her. "You good, Brooklyn?" she asked.

"Why you asking me that? Don't I look good?" Brooklyn stepped back to flaunt her cut-off shirt (which exposed her belly ring), her new J's, and her hairstyle.

"You know what I mean. Looks like you're really enjoying that drink. Is it spiked?" Vanessa asked with a raised eyebrow.

"Naw, I doubt it. It has a little kick, but I don't think so," Brooklyn answered, holding up the cup as if looking at it from the outside could tell the potency of the drink inside.

Vanessa shook her head and said, "Come here, girl," and dragged Brooklyn to a spot where they could sit and talk with more privacy.

"B, you don't look like your normal self. I'm not telling you what to do, but I want you to know that there are tons of drugs here. When I first got here, I walked into a cloud of smoke that for sure wasn't tobacco." Vanessa gave her bff a look like, "You know what I mean."

"I do feel a little off. And at first, I thought it was because I didn't eat anything. And it's crazy hot in here! I feel a little light-headed."

"Justin!" Vanessa shouted, gesturing him to come over to where she and Brooklyn were. "Please get B some water and something to eat that looks decent."

"Ok," Justin responded. "You want anything for yourself?"

"I'm good, thanks," Vanessa responded quickly.

Justin returned with a slice of pizza and a bottled water. Brooklyn scoffed it down. Vanessa took a tour of the house to see what was *really* going on there and to make sure none of her underclassmen friends was being taken advantage of. She saw Bobby near the staircase talking to one of the cheerleaders. "Bobby!" yelled Vanessa.

Bobby told the girl he was speaking with to give him a minute. "What's up, V?" Bobby asked.

"Dude, what's with all the drugs in your house? It's crazy." Vanessa demanded an answer, clearly by the placement of her hands on her hips.

"Take it easy, Vanessa. Relax. No one is making you do anything you don't want to. I didn't bring the drugs, but it's not that serious. A little weed, some spiked punch... It's nothing, relax!" "Relax? Brooklyn is over there about to puke. And had we not shown up, who knows what would have happened? You need to know what's in your house and who is hangin' here. I saw Ryan and I'm not stupid, I know he sells."

"Well, I'm not buying, but I can't control what others do. Party or break out, but don't be a party pooper. Everyone is just chilling, so take it easy." Bobby headed back over to the girl he was talking to, who was now talking to a football player.

Vanessa headed back over to Justin and Brooklyn. "How are you feeling now, Brook?"

"Better. Thank you for snatching me up. I was getting a little light-headed, and didn't even think anything about the drink."

"Yeah. There's alcohol, weed, and pills here. God knows what else. I'm scared to go to the bathroom 'cause I feel like I'm going to walk in on someone hooking up. We need to get out of here, pronto." Without further comment, they all made their way to the door.

Bobby saw his friends advance for the exit and he made a dash to catch up to them. "Hey, guys, why y'all leaving?"

"Isn't it obvious?" Vanessa asked with a scowl on her face. "You're playing yourself, Bobby. You're better than this. Why you letting these upper-classmen and total strangers in your house do whatever they want?"

"It's not like that. We're all having a good time. I'm in control of this. Plus, I don't want to look corny telling people to not get high. That's them, not me."

They all looked at Bobby with faces that said, *That's a soft move, bro.*

"Hey, Bobby, that's on you. We out! And, oh, yeah ... Don't drink the punch, it's spiked," Brooklyn added.

As the three of them left, Bobby looked down into his cup in disbelief with a sense of helplessness. Vanessa, Brooklyn, and Justin headed home. They dropped Brooklyn off first to make sure she got in the house safely. And then they speed off.

There was an awkward silence in the EZ-Ride car Justin had ordered on the app.

"What's up with you, Jus? Why so quiet?"

"Just thinking about all the trouble I would be in if I threw a party like that."

"You would never do that. You have more sense than to disrespect your mother's house, or yourself, for that matter," Vanessa confidently commented.

"Thanks for thinking highly of me, V, but I feel like my good-guy image is a disadvantage sometimes. Girls like guys that have a bad-boy image and lots of swagger. Take, for example, the last guy you dated."

"Hold-up!" Vanessa interrupted. "You know my parents don't let me date yet. You mean the last guy I *liked*," she said, making a clear distinction.

"'Not dated, Ms. I'm-too-young to get caught up with that just yet. I meant '*liked*,'" Justin re-stated with clarity. "He was like your school bae for a minute. You were soft on him, for sure. I saw you wearing his letterman jacket. That was a big deal! You know I'm telling the truth. Whatever happened with that?"

"He turned out to be a creep. He was always asking me to come over so we could Netflix and chill. I know what that means. I was like, 'Let's go to the park and chill,'" Vanessa shot back with a frown, shaking her head. "I got tired of the constant invite to his house. It was corny after a while. I was like, 'Dude, if we're getting to know each other, let's talk. Let's hang out in groups. Keep it PG.' A week later, he got with Lisa. I saw her wearing his jacket and they were holding hands in gym."

"Whoa, he was speeding, huh?"

"Speeding ain't the word. I don't get down like that. I guess he didn't get the memo."

They both laughed. Then, an awkward silence ensued.

"I would treat you better," Jason broke the silence and offered sincerely.

The rest of the ride back to Vanessa's was quiet, and all so awkward. When the car arrived at her house, Justin smiled and quickly blurted out, "Crazy night, huh?"

Vanessa got out and smiled back. "Later, Jus."

"Later, Vanessa." The driver and Justin watched and waited until V entered her house safely. Then they drove away...

HOW ABOUT YOU?

1. Have you ever been to a friend's party where there were drugs and/or alcohol? If so, how did you handle it?

_____

_____

_____

2. Have you ever had to discourage a friend from using drugs and/or alcohol at a party or in or out of school? If so, what did you do?

_____

_____

_____

3. If you knew someone needed help, what steps could you take to get him/her the help he/she needed?

_____

_____

_____

4. If you use drugs and/or alcohol and need help, is there someone you could talk to? If so, who? If not, would you consider going to your school counselor?

_____

_____

_____

13

#ITHAPPENEDAGAIN

Weeks went by and there was no news from Brooklyn and the gang about any chatroom drama—or any mention of John. Everyone was preoccupied with finals, football and soccer playoffs, and state testing. The squad hadn't really hung out lately due to all these competing obligations. On their way to the bus stop one morning, Vanessa asked Brooklyn about John. Brooklyn responded with a look of disbelief.

"Why do you ask?" she snapped.

"Because we're friends, and I am interested in knowing what's going on with you."

"I'm good. John has been MIA, and we haven't chatted in a while."

"Don't you find that strange, Brooklyn? How he disappeared without saying anything?" Vanessa inquired sympathetically.

"I guess so. But he said his father was an overprotected popular athlete that moved around a lot."

"Yeah, that sounds like a great story for being mysterious and secretive," Vanessa responded.

"There you go. That's the Vanessa I know," Brooklyn said with frustration. "You were just asking so you could say something slick."

"That's not it at all. I just find all of this off. It's not my intention to fade you. I just want to have your back and to tell you the truth—even if it's not what you want to hear."

As more students lined up for the bus, they changed the subject. Their bus ride was pretty pleasant. Almost like the old days.

When they arrived at school, everyone was immediately ushered to the auditorium.

"What's going on?" Vanessa asked her volleyball coach.

"It's a special assembly. Something just happened that needs to be shared with everyone," Coach G. responded in a serious tone.

As they walked in, Vanessa was looking around trying to figure out what to expect and which familiar faces to sit next to. Mr. Jones was holding the microphone and Big Nate's dad was standing next to him with an intense look.

Whatever it is, it can't be good, Vanessa thought.

The students settled in their seats. And on this day, in particular, all of the faculty members were extra-strict about students *not* taking out their phones. Vanessa had already witnessed two students' phones being confiscated for having them out. *This is different,* Vanessa told herself. *What could have happened?*

The assembly began like a normal one. Mr. Jones greeted everyone, and then congratulated the girls' volleyball team and Coach G. on the big win in the championship game. After the cheering and the trophy presentation, Mr. Jones introduced Community Police Officer Kimble who demanded everyone's undivided attention. An immediate silence fell over the students.

Brooklyn, Justin, and Vanessa were looking at each other like, "Oh boy, another neighborhood safety speech." However, the moment Officer Kimble started speaking, everyone realized it wasn't the same old message. This was where it went different.

Officer Kimble mentioned an incident that had just happened at a rival high school. In fact, it was the school that Vanessa's team had just defeated in the championship game. He spoke about a girl that was abducted, and when Vanessa heard the name Kim, she was stricken with grief. *I just played against her, this is not happening.*

Everyone was speechless; they couldn't believe what they were hearing. The entire school was sitting on the edge of their seats hanging on every word that Officer Kimble shared. Apparently, this older guy, online, was impersonating a high school student from the private school. *No way, no way, no way. Don't say Hillside Academy for the Gifted and Talented,* Vanessa stressed in her mind.

"Hillside Academy for the Gifted and Talented," the officer mentioned. Justin looked at Vanessa, who looked at Brooklyn, who looked at DJ, who looked at Bobby and Jason, who were looking at their phones' playlists and anticipating lunch. Some things never changed.

The student body sat in utter disbelief as Officer Kimble finished the story. Vanessa and her group realized how eerily similar it was to how John became friends with them in the chatroom. A rush of questions flooded Vanessa's mind. *What if I had given up on looking out for Brooklyn? What if Brooklyn didn't have friends that cared enough to question things? What if no one supported me in MY doubts?*

Vanessa started crying uncontrollably. She looked at Brooklyn, thought about Kim and Giselle, and just couldn't control her sorrow. She was so overwhelmed with grief. She felt that this could have easily been Brooklyn—or herself! She also couldn't imagine what Kim's family was going through at that moment.

Mr. Jones tried to calm everyone down by sharing more. "This is certainly a time to grieve and support each other as a community. If you have any information that may help locate Kim, or need to talk for whatever reason, please be encouraged to visit your guidance counselor."

As the days went by, more and more information came out. Evidently, Kim had given this guy, whom she didn't know, her home address. He had managed to get her to tell him when she was alone. He had also figured out her parents' work schedule and convinced Kim to invite him over to her house. The Cyber Department at the police station shared this on a return visit to the school.

This time, both Officer Kimble and a lead investigator from the Cyber Department came to the school. They addressed students in their health classes so they could share more information in an intimate setting and allow for questions. The cyber investigator brought a chart as a visual aid and spoke about some of the things online predators do to gain people's trust. He explained that predators:

Make you feel comfortable

Work really hard to blend in by showing interest in what you show interest in

Are typically kind and friendly

Act very social while protecting their identity

Are extremely easy-going

Never show frustration or anger

Vanessa was in deep thought and shock. *This was John in every way. He never once took offense with my questions. He was always ready with an answer. He was very complimentary online and spoke about things that everyone liked.*

Just then, Vanessa's cellphone pinged. She looked at her screen. There posted was 💔, followed by a message that read, "You were my first choice. J."

HOW ABOUT YOU?

1. Have you ever experienced getting attention from someone online who seemed a little suspicious? If so, why do you think you felt that way?

   _____

   _____

   _____

2. What do you think you can you do to guard against this happening to you or a friend?

   _____

   _____

   _____

3. Has this story given you second thoughts as to how you are using social media?

   _____

   _____

   _____

4. Has this story made you think more about the concept of "trust"?

   _____

   _____

   _____

5. Has this story compelled you to think about what it means to be a friend and who your true friends really are?

_____

_____

_____

6. Has this story made you think deeper about the type of friend that you are to others?

_____

_____

_____

7. Finally, how can social media be used productively to help support some of the positive choices that you described above? Please share your ideas how.

_____

_____

_____

In the end, we will
remember not the
words of our
enemies, but the
silence of our
friends.

Martin Luther King Jr.

BEFORE YOU POST...

T·H·I·N·K·

IS IT... | **TRUE** HELPFUL INSPIRING NECESSARY KIND

Connect with Cory

Let's Connect!

Any questions or comments about the book can be sent directly to Cory Alexander at info@followedthebook.com. Or you can send a message through the social media platforms listed below.

- Twitter.com/FollowedTheBook
- Instagram.com/AuthorCoryAlexander
- Facebook.com/FollowedTheBook

Experience exclusive content on the website – FollowedTheBook.com. Stay connected with Vanessa, Brooklyn and Justin as they enter their sophomore year and much more!

Just because the book is over, doesn't mean the discussion has to end. Join the Followed Facebook group to discuss the book or issues like social media, online safety, and cyber bullying.